A Giant First-Start® Reader

This easy reader contains only 54 words,
repeated often to help the young reader develop
word recognition and interest in reading.

Basic word list for *Monster Party*

a	games	now
all	gets	of
and	go	party
at	happy	play
away	has	plays
big	have	plenty
birthday	having	present
bring	he	presents
but	heavy	says
cake	his	scat
come	ice	she
cream	is	sister
does	it	the
eat	little	they
eats	mad	things
friends	monster	what
fun	noisy	why
furry	not	wins

Monster Party

by Patsy Jensen

illustrated by Patrick Girouard

Troll Associates

Little Monster is having a party.

Little Monster is having a birthday party.

All his friends come. They bring presents.

They play games.

They play party games.

Little Monster wins!

They eat plenty of things.

They eat plenty of cake and ice cream.

Little Monster has fun.

All his friends have fun.

But Little Monster gets mad.

Why is he mad?

His little sister is at the party.

"Scat!" he says.

But she does not go away.

She plays party games.

She wins!

"Scat!" he says.

But she does not go away.

She eats plenty of things.

"Scat!" he says.

But she does not go away.

She eats plenty of cake and ice cream.

"Scat!" he says.

But she does not go away.

Now Little Monster is happy.

Why is he happy?

He gets a present.
The present is big.

The present is heavy.

The present is noisy.

The present is furry.

What is it?

Happy Birthday, Little Monster!